# Roger's Revelation

# An Emma: Ancestor's Tales Vignette

# By Paula Shablo

This story is dedicated to my brother, Frank Shablo.
He would as enthusiastically embrace evidence of the
afterlife as Emma's brother, Fred. I'll bet he'd haul my
bags for me, too. I love you, Frank!

# Author's Note

Emma Knight Kramer sees ghosts.

It's not what she would have chosen as her claim to fame, but she has accepted that it is her lot in life to see and speak to the spirits of either her own ancestors or those who were associated with them in their lifetimes. They tell her stories of the past to pass on to the living, and sometimes present her with mysteries to be solved in order for them to move on peacefully in their afterlives.

It is not an easy calling.

Like many of us—probably most of us—Emma would prefer to hear a story, make note of it and move on with her life. She would like a story with a beginning, a middle and an end.

While most of the stories she hears have those elements, there have been many that were unresolved. Those have had to be researched and questioned and documented. Some have ended well enough, but some have been tragic.

Some are still unresolved.

Up until now, though, Emma has never encountered a story that would adversely affect anyone still living.

Sure, we probably all have an ancient relation who was a notorious stage coach bandit or a dance hall girl. But
those things are so far back in our lineage that we just shrug and thank the lucky stars that times have certainly changed since then.

Not so the visit by Roger that follows. Most of the family members are still among the living, and the situation will not be easily dealt with.

This is only the beginning.

# An Excerpt from the Diary of Emma Knight Kramer

April 9, 1988

Dear Diary,

What a weird day!

At one point today, I really thought I was going to get to see all ghosts. You know, any ghosts, not just those who are in some way related to me.

And it was exciting!

But it wasn't the case after all.

I guess I should just start at the beginning.

I got a call earlier this week from the paper. They asked me to attend—get this! —a Junior High School dance.

It turns out the dance was not one of the usual deals like Sadie Hawkins or the Snow Ball. One of the students was in a car accident, and the kids asked to host a fund-raiser to help with medical expenses.

I thought that was pretty sweet, but I don't write for the paper, so I wasn't sure why they wanted me to go.

It turned out they wanted a photographer present to take pictures of the event, and then the school asked if said photographer could also do dance-night photos.

I figured what the heck? It's a decent paycheck from the paper, and although I plan to donate part of my proceeds from the individual dance night photos, after paying my expenses I'll probably make a decent amount of profit.

(Just so you know, Diary—sure wish I could get the photo op for Prom. Then I could really make some money! But it seems like they never hire locally!)

Anyway…

Jacob is on night shift, so the twins went to Grandma's house for the night.

Let me just add really quick how lucky I am to have such a great mom, and how grateful I am that she lives nearby so I can take advantage of her like this!

I got Fred to agree to help move backdrops and equipment by bribing him with lunch at Taco Time and a promise to let him drive. He got his learner's permit in January—birthday month—and I can't…I *just can't* believe it.

We went over to the school, and—did I say Junior High? Well, it was when I went there, but it's a Middle School now, grades six through eight. Why are they having dances? They're babies!

(Not like we didn't have mixers every Friday afternoon when I was in Junior High, which was grades seven through nine. But WE weren't babies. Right?)

Anyway, we went over and set up the backdrop and tripod for the camera. Then we went to Taco Time and chowed down on not-good-for-us but delicious crispy bean burritos and soft combo burritos and root beer.

Then I made good on the harder part of my promise and let Fred drive us around. He took us through the tunnels, giggling with glee while I cowered in the passenger seat.

Look, Diary, I know you're judging me right now, but I don't care. I grew up in this town, I've gone through those tunnels countless times, and I hate it every single time. I don't like the idea that I am zipping through the bombed-out interior of a mountainside, tons of rock and soil just waiting to cave in on me, okay? Plus—the walls! They are so close. You can get from here to there without going through them at all, so why? Why?

Yep. Emmaline Kramer, chicken. That's me.

Fred wasn't up for a Middle School dance, big old High School kid that he is now, so I dropped him off at home and headed back to the school. I figured I could canvas the auditorium set-up and figure out where to take shots for the paper.

Their reporter would be there later, so I had the place to myself.

As I was headed down the hall, there he was—Roger Peters!

And I just knew that everything had changed for me. I could see a ghost who was an old classmate of mine!

"Roger?" I cried.

"Emma?" Roger looked as shocked as I felt. "You can really see me?"

"I—I can! I don't know how, but—"

"He said you would," Roger mused.

"Who?" I was still too stunned to give this serious consideration. I could see Roger, who was—

"My grandfather. Your great-grandfather. He told me you'd see me."

"Your—my—what?"

*Huh?*

"Roger, what are you going on about?" I demanded. Had he really just insinuated that my great-grandfather was his grandfather?

Flabbergasted.

"Wow," Roger said. "I didn't believe it. I figured you'd just walk right past me—or *though* me, maybe. That's always a fun possibility."

"Huh?"

"I didn't plan what to say!" Roger cried. "I thought he was having me on, you know? No one sees ghosts!"

"Roger, you've known me since, like, fourth grade! How can you even say that?"

"Well, obviously, *you* saw them!" Roger back-peddled.

"Well, obviously, *you* didn't believe that."

Roger pursed his lips. "Well," he sighed. "I did, and I didn't. I mean, I didn't really *want* to believe there were any ghosts."

I remembered then how he'd died. Rather harshly, I said, "Yeah. I'll bet you didn't."

"Well, *obviously*, that didn't work out so great for me, now, did it?"

I felt bad then. I'm a jerk.

"Come on," I told him. "I'm getting ready for a gig."

We went into the auditorium and I began my preparations.

"Okay, spill," I commanded. "Why can I see you?"

"You remember my parents, Emma?" Roger asked.

"Well, yeah," I replied. "I still see them all the time."

"You do?" He looked surprised. "How are they?"

"Fine."

Well, they looked fine the last time I saw them, anyway, but what do I know?

"Good." He sighed deeply. "Good."

I waited. Finally, I prompted him, "But?"

"Kinda turns out," he shrugged, "My Dad is just the guy married to my mother who never knew she had a thing for older guys."

"Wh—what?"

"Yeah, my older brother is his, and my younger sister, too. But me?" Roger held out his hands, palms up. "Product of an 'illicit liaison'."

"What are you saying, Roger? Your mother had an affair?"

I know Roger's mother, okay? She's this mousy little woman who looks at the ground when you talk to her. She has a nervous giggle and looks like she might bolt for the door if you cough in her presence. I am still beyond shocked.

"Yeah," Roger replied, his eyes wide with incredulity. "I know, right? It couldn't happen."

"Well, who says it did?"

Roger sighed hard and shook his head. "You see me, right?"

"Well, yeah, but—"

"Ever see anyone else who wasn't related to you?"

"Well, no, but—"

"This guy comes up to me, okay? Says, 'Now why'd you go and do something so foolish, boy?' and I was, like, 'Who the hell are you?' I never saw this guy before in my life, right? And he says, 'Mind your manners, sonny Jim. I'm your grandpa.'"

"Oh…kay," I said.

"And I told him he was wrong, my grandpa is like, I don't know, seventy-something and living in Heber, Utah. And he said, no, I was wrong, that was my brother's and sister's grandpa, but *my* grandpa was standing right there with me."

Diary, I was floored, but still befuddled. Roger had said this man—his grandfather—was my great-grandfather, too. At least, I was pretty sure that was what he'd said. (Turns out it was.) Now, I never knew my Dad's grandfather, but my Grandma's father died only a year before she did, so he was a pretty constant figure in my life up until recently.

No one had ever mentioned him having a grandson my age!

"I don't get it," I admitted. "He—what? Met you at the gate? That's impossible. You've been gone longer than he has."

And that's true. Roger left this plane while we were still in High School. Over a decade ago!

Roger looked flummoxed. "This was…I don't know, Em. I got no real perception of time passage, ya know? I'd have to say it was recent, our little chat. You know, compared with how long I've been just kickin' it over here."

"Kicking it?"

"Hey, there's just…" he grimaced, and looked at his feet. "I got nothin' here. I really messed up." He looked up at me and grinned. "And, to be clear? I ain't seen no gate!"

"Oh, I—" I could feel myself blushing. "That was just a figure of speech. I have no idea…"

Roger grinned again, sheepish. "Yeah, you know the saying, 'if I knew then what I know now'?"

"Yeah."

"True story."

I guess I need to take a step back in time and do some explaining. It was probably 1975, or maybe '76, I can't remember—and I certainly didn't want to ask Roger! We were in High School, anyway, and it was the old building, so it can't have been any later than that.

Some of the older students drove to school. I was one of the bus kids, myself, too young for a license, but old enough to be in drivers' education class. That was the class I had with Roger that year. There were four of us, and poor Roger was the only male in the car. He didn't dare make a "women drivers" remark—we'd have had his head. Even the instructor was a woman, but she was a tough old bird, and there weren't any kids crazy enough to give her any trouble.

Roger was a quiet kid. Never caused any trouble; never had a bad word to say about anyone. Wherever he was, he was "background", if you know what I mean. I suppose if he'd been a girl, one might have called him a wallflower, sexist as that sounds.

He was *quiet*. He probably went to a great deal of trouble not to do anything that might draw attention to himself.

He had an older brother, Darren, who was an impressive athlete, and I guess Roger could have lived in the large shadow cast by his sibling. Truth is, though, I never once saw the two of them together. If the town wasn't so small, with most everyone knowing everyone else, no one would have known they were even related, let alone brothers.

Darren drove an old pickup to school every day. A Senior that year, he sometimes left early to go to an after-school job, and other times stayed quite late participating in the sport of the season. Football, basketball, wrestling—he did it all.

Roger rode the bus.

That says a lot right there, I think.

Darren, like most other guys his age, had a gun rack in his truck. There were rifles on the rack, ammunition in the glove compartment—and probably in the guns—and likely a nice assortment of hunting knives and other gear behind and under the seats.

It's Wyoming. No one gave a though to all the guns in racks in the unlocked vehicles in the parking lot, guns that belonged to both students and teachers. There might have been a more prominent display of firearms during hunting season, when folks might be expected to head for the hills as soon as the last bell rang, but there were plenty enough all year 'round.

Now, as I said, my time-frame is not exact. It may have been fall of '75 or spring of '76 when Roger left the car we'd been driving for our driver's ed class and walked off around the back of the school building.

Mrs. McKay watched him go, frowning. We were supposed to go back inside, all of us, but she didn't call for him to come back. She just said, "Huh! We all have a bad drive in us, girls. Remember that."

And Roger had really *had* a bad driving day. Truth to tell, we all had. "Marshall" McKay—so called because she reminded some wit from the past of Marshall Dillon of Gunsmoke fame, God knows why—was quite the task-master, and on that particular day had decided to take us up on the dirt road leading to the cemetery for a lesson on driving smoothly.

She kept an item in the car that she called her little nesting egg. It looked like a snow globe with a golf ball on a tee inside. In order to pass the smooth drive test, you had to maneuver the car over the bumps and ruts without knocking the ball off the tee.

I wish to this day that I'd had the nerve to ask her to do it herself, and prove it was possible. God knows none of us were able to do it.

By the time we came back to school that day, I had chewed a nice bloody hole in my lip, Susan was grinding her teeth, Bonita's eyes were red-rimmed and teary, and Roger's face was a stony mask. We had all been berated for our seriously-lacking skills, and we were all silently plotting to push the old "Marshall" into a mud puddle.

She had driven us back, all the time reminding us that it was imperative not to let a stressful situation distract us from the task at hand. "That," she declared, "is the primary cause of accidents—distractions in times of stress." She was, after all, only preparing us to go forth fully armed with a defensive plan against the inevitable.

Oh, dear diary, I'm making her sound like an awful person, and she wasn't. She was just tough. She really did want us to be good, defensive drivers who pay attention under difficult circumstances, and we live in Wyoming, home of I-80 and the most dangerous winter driving conditions in the country.

We are good drivers, those of us who passed her class. It takes a lot to rattle us. I moan and fuss about driving—I'm not a person who enjoys it, honestly—but I can do it and do it well.

You NEVER forget that stupid nesting egg.

Anyway, for whatever reason, that last driving lesson was the straw that broke Roger Peters' back.

He went to the back parking lot, took his brother's truck, drove down to the river and shot himself in the head.

Mrs. McKay resigned.

She blamed herself. She was too hard on him, she said. She wondered how many other students she had driven to self-harm, or drinking, or drugs. I never saw such a case of self-abuse!

Well…*Roger*. Yeah.

But…it was awful to watch a formally tough person just fall apart like that. She went from a robust 150 pounds to a scrawny 100. She wrinkled like a prune in a manner of weeks. Within the year, she had a heart attack and passed away.

I haven't seen her. It's not likely I ever will. But I wish I could. I wish I could tell her it wasn't ever her fault.

Yes, I just admitted to you that we wanted to push her in a mud puddle. But what happened to her? Never!

Talk about a "bad drive day"!

Darren found his truck missing a few hours later, having gone from class to one sort of sport practice or other. He called the cops, and a police report was filed. Then he caught a ride with a teammate and went gallivanting around a bit before going home, looking haphazardly for his truck, but mostly just goofing off until his parents would be home, so he could tell them all about his misfortune.

Roger's sister had an after-school piano lesson, and then went to a neighbor's house to babysit for a while.

The Peters family didn't assemble until nearly seven that evening, and that was the first time anyone realized that Roger hadn't come home.

As I recall, phone calls to neighbors and friends were the beginning of the search, and then people started looking. The police speculated that Roger was probably the one who had taken Darren's truck.

We weren't well acquainted with the family, so none of us were involved in searching, and all I can go on is the talk around town that followed.

I'm not sure where along the Green River Roger had parked to do the deed, but it's a river, my dear diary. It goes on forever in both directions.

It was hours before he was found.

So—were we, the driver's education class and instructor—really the last ones to see him alive?

Oh, the questions!

And now, here he was, watching me load film and choose the backdrop, shoot a couple of practice Polaroid shots to make sure the lighting was going to work. Adjustments were made.

He stepped into the last shot, and I never noticed, even when I peeled the paper backing from the photo after my timer went off. I didn't even look at that one, because the one before it had satisfied me; the backdrop and lighting would work fine. I just set the stack of instant photos aside, and later shoved them all into my bag.

More on that later, but—let's just say I can't wait to call Sasha.

It was hard to work with Roger watching. Like I said, I had so many questions and no nerve to ask them.

After making sure my smaller camera was loaded and that the flash was functioning, I blurted, "Okay, Roger! What happened?"

Ghosts can sigh. Roger did so, heavily. "It was a rotten day," he said.

"Not just for you," I countered. I was thinking of Mrs. McKay, how things ended for her.

"No, of course not," Roger agreed. He appeared to be thinking hard about how to go on. Finally, he said, "It was just the *last* rotten day, I guess."

I didn't know what to say to that, so I just waited.

He sighed again. "I don't know why it suddenly seemed to be so...*much*," he said. "I had so many things I wanted to do, so many things I wanted to say. But I could never seem to make myself do anything about it." He looked at me, his face so earnest, so...so *young*.

My heart was breaking, dear diary.

I didn't *know* Roger. Okay? He was in that one class, and he never said much of anything. He was just there, in the background at school, a face that I recognized in the crowd on one occasion and looked right past on another.

How did I miss the *person* behind the face?

I feel like a monster.

"It wasn't the driving," he continued. "Honestly, she did that to everyone. That dumb nesting egg trick? Darren told me about it. I knew she'd do it sooner or later."

"I hated that dang golf ball," I agreed.

"I didn't do any worse than anyone else, I knew that! But…God, it just pissed me off, Emma! It was like this…what do you call it? Analogy? No…epiphany! Right? Like every stupid thing I ever tried, ruts and bumps and falling golf balls, and I was never gonna get it right. I was never going to *excel*."

"I—"

"You ever hear of middle child syndrome?"

"Well…"

Should I have told him Melody, our middle child, used to say she'd risen above it—even though she never got an "A" in English class like Dana and I did? But it was her best excuse for the night she ran off to a kegger and got falling-down-puking-in-her-hair drunk?

Nah, I don't think so. Because Mel is a freaking rock star—a *real* one.

"The middle child is the problem child," he explained. "Or the invisible child, if he's not making himself a problem. I guess that would be more me."

"Why? Because Darren was such an athlete?" I asked.

"Oh…I don't know. Not really," Roger said. "I was always real proud of my brother. But he barely knew I was around when we were at school. I mean, at home, he was great. But around his buddies? I was a non-entity."

I thought of all the times I had ignored my sisters at school and cringed.

Roger looked alarmed and said, "Stop that! He wasn't being mean to me, he just…we just…didn't move in the same circles?" He shrugged.

"Really?" I cried. "I think Mel might take a different view of that. I was just…"

Roger nodded knowingly. "What *you* were doing," he said, "was trying to limit their exposure to your…um… eccentricities."

"You've got quite the vocabulary, there, buddy," I told him. All the while I was thinking, *was that what I was doing?*

I suppose it was, you know. Grandma called me out on it, a long time ago.

But how had he figured it out? Are people smarter when they're dead? Does the afterlife give you special insights?

"My brother wasn't mean. He was talented and popular, and I wasn't. That's all. And my sister was adorable and sweet and the youngest and the only girl and we all loved her best. Exactly as we should have, do you see?"

"Sure," I agreed. We had been the same way with Matthew. It was different with Freddie; he was so much younger it was like loving your *own* baby, at least for me. We were still little girls when Matthew was the baby, and inclined to indulge, rather than nurture.

Does that make sense? Oh well, who are you gonna tell, dear diary?

"Anyway, ever since we started sophomore year, I just felt cut off from everything. Like I was standing outside and watching everything through a window." Roger cast his eyes toward the ceiling, and then looked back at me. "A window with bars," he added.

"Roger—"

"I couldn't get in," he said. "I couldn't get out. No one could hear me calling. I felt like I was screaming, and no sound was coming out."

"I'm so sorry," I said. "You never seemed…"

Seemed what, I wondered. Sad? Angry? What did it take to make you drive down to the river, anyway?

"I don't know what I was," Roger said. "I think I was tired."

"You were, what? Fifteen? Sixteen?"

"Fifteen," he replied. "And tired. Done to death, I guess." Suddenly he burst out laughing.

"Roger!" I admonished.

"Ah, I don't know how long it has been, but I reckon it's been long enough to look back and laugh a little," he told me. "If I could have done that then—laugh a little—I might be helping you develop film later. But everything seemed so *serious*."

I felt like crying. Or cussing a little. Maybe both.

"Anyway, I wandered around, and wondered how things were going, but I couldn't make myself go to the house. Not then. I figure I caused some trouble."

"You think?"

"So, what happened?"

Well, that was direct!

And how do you even answer that?

Darren was destroyed, I remember. He wouldn't let anyone deal with the truck, sold it right where it stood after hauling water from the river to wash it out. The cops, the crews, they couldn't stop him. "Get your evidence and get out!" he'd yelled and started filling buckets. "*My* brother*! Mine!*"

Manny Ortega told my father this, and I overheard. He said that truck had never been so clean, probably not since it was fresh off the assembly line. Every drop of blood scrubbed away with detergent and river water.

He never drove it again. Wouldn't even start the engine.

I don't know who bought it, but it was never seen again; not in town, not on the freeway, maybe not in the whole county.

People looked for it, you know. Everyone said so. People are a strange lot.

Jerry Hendrickson told me that Darren took the guns and beat them to a pulp with a sledge hammer, then buried them on the spot where the truck was found. He said he was glad the guy had had the presence of mind to make sure they weren't loaded, or he'd probably have been injured.

I suppose there might have been a marker of some sort placed at the site, but I don't know where they found the truck. I was never one to stop to look at accident sites, not on the freeway or anywhere else, and I certainly don't seek them out.

Where their parents were through all this, I couldn't tell you. I'm sure they were wrecked by it, but my folks didn't move in the same circles. Hearsay is all they had to go on, just like me. Not that they shared much of what they heard, of course. It wasn't dinner table conversation.

Dana was in the same class with Roger's sister; her name is Margo. I guess she didn't come back to school right away, and when she did, she'd lost a lot of weight. She didn't talk much anymore and cried a lot.

I can imagine.

At some point we learned that his mousy little mother wasn't coping well at all and finally broke down and had to have a short stay in Evanston before she could get a handle on things.

I guess I should mention, diary, that Evanston is where the mental hospital is. Everyone knows it, but I never let you in on that, did I?

Roger was waiting for me to say something. It's not like I could tell him all the things I just told you, right? Those things all darted through my mind, but…

"It was a big funeral," I told Roger. "It seemed like the whole town was there. Your family got a lot of support."

This is the absolute truth. There were school assemblies and support groups and suicide counseling, too.

Until then, I never knew there was such a thing as suicide counseling.

"Well, that's good, I guess," Roger said.

I'd said as little as possible; I couldn't have said most of those things out loud.

He sighed again. "I just hope no one blamed Marshall McKay," he added.

*No one except Mrs. McKay*, I thought. She never stopped blaming herself.

"Since hers was the class I walked out of. Kinda," he continued, and then looked me straight in the eye.

I said nothing. *Nothing.*

What could he discern from my silence, I wonder?

Look, they come to tell me their stories. Most are so old that any information I give them can't harm them. But everyone else in Roger's story so far is still alive, dang it.

He doesn't need to know. Not now.

But—

"Didn't you go?" I asked.

"Go?"

"To the funeral."

Curiosity gets the best of me sometimes.

"Emma…" Roger looked confused and frustrated. "I don't know how I could have. No concept of time, remember?"

"But—"

"Listen, I remember taking the truck. Darren left the keys in it, and I just jumped in and took it, and drove.

"I went down to the river and just sat there, you know? Thinking it was just too much. Thinking I didn't want to do it anymore.

"I remember the gun. I made sure it was loaded. I remember moving to the passenger side of the seat, so I wouldn't mess up the place where Darren sits. I didn't want him to be mad at me.

"Just when I pulled the trigger, I thought, *oh, shit, I should have done this outside*. And then…then I was just…nowhere."

"Huh?"

Nowhere? What does *that* mean?

Diary, I have been doing this for years now, and no one has ever told me much about where they go. It's big. It's vast. It's empty. Or it's full of people.

That's specific, right?

No one seems to think of it as Heaven or Hell. It's just a space.

It's frustrating, because I want to *know!*

"It was like a bank of really thick fog, and I was just walking," Roger said. "I was all alone for the longest time."

*Well, that sucks!* I thought.

"And then along comes this guy, claiming to be my grandpa. Jeez, Emma. Do you know him?"

"Um…you never told me his name, Roger."

"Uh…wow! He didn't tell me! He just said he had a son named Ezra, and that Ezra was my real father."

I gasped. "My mom's uncle Ezra is your *father?*" I fairly shrieked. "But he's—cripes! He's really *old!* He's like 70 or something."

So, I'm standing there looking at the clock—people were going to start showing up any minute now! — and doing some mental arithmetic.

"Okay, nah, that's not so bad," I said. "He'd have been in his forties or so."

Roger grimaced. "I guess," he said. "But my mom was like twenty-two when I was born. Gross."

I shrugged. "It happens," I said. "But—did your Dad ever know?"

"I have no idea." Roger sighed. "I hope not."

I squeezed my eyes shut, frustrated. "Dang it!" I cried. "I wish *we* had known. Maybe—"

"Things might have been different?" Roger shook his head. "How? You'd have been my best friend? I mean…ah, who knows?"

I know I made some sort of awful face and a snorting noise at that point, because... yeah! Who knows? Would things have been better, or worse? And what was the point of speculating?

"Okay, so Great-Grandpa came to you and told you this," I said. "How did *he* know?"

"He told me Ezra told him about the affair, and later told him about me. So, I guess they both always knew..."

"Well, what the hell," I grumbled. "He knew the whole time?"

"I don't know. I guess."

"I wonder if the Great-Grandmother knew," I mused.

"I didn't see any grandmother," Roger told me.

People were arriving to prepare for the dance; students, teachers, some parent chaperones, all carrying various items to set up the refreshments tables.

I had to pay attention to the activity around me, but I didn't want to stop this conversation.

Not that there was anyone there who hadn't seen me "talking to myself" at one time or another.

It's a small town. People know me, whether I like it or not.

I wondered where the great-grandmother was, and why she wasn't with the great-grandfather.

After all the difficulty Manuelita had had finding her Juan Gonzales, I desperately hoped my great-grands were reunited.

Did they have unresolved issues that would keep them apart?

Oooh. How about an illegitimate grandson?

My stomach hurt then.

"Look around, Roger," I said, surveying the gymnasium. "See anyone you know?"

Punch bowls were being placed and filled. Trays were being filled with a large variety of cookies. Stacks of napkins, paper plates and paper cups were strategically placed along the tables.

Roger gave the working people a cursory glance, indifferent.

Certainly, I didn't expect him to recognize any of the students working on final decorations; they were all easily fifteen years younger than I. But a couple of the teachers were the same we'd studied under, and there were a few parents I recognized from church and other public gathering places.

"I guess maybe a couple of people look familiar," Roger said. "Who cares, though? They can't see me, and I never meant anything to them."

Okay, I had to ask. "Why are you here, Roger? What made you decide to seek me out?"

"The old man told me you could see me," Roger said. "He said I could talk to you."

"Okay, yes, I can see you. But what do you want to say, Roger? I mean, do you want me to tell someone something? Do you want to go see your parents?"

"What? No!" Roger looked horrified.

I found this distressing. A dozen years had passed, maybe as many as a baker's dozen. Had he never found himself at his house, looking in on his family? I stared at him accusingly and asked him that straight out.

He tightened his lips and blinked rapidly. "I have," he admitted. "I barely knew them; my sis...my sister was a woman, not the little girl I remember." He stared at me. "She has a daughter!"

"My sister was in her class," I said. "She has two kids herself."

"But how?" Roger cried. "I haven't—I didn't...I mean, it can't be!"

"Can't be what?" I asked. "Did you think time would just stop when *you* did? That nothing would change while you walked in the fog?"

"I don't know..."

"There's a reason they say, 'Life goes on', Roger," I said, hoping I didn't sound too unkind. "They say it because it is true."

"Well, I know that, Emma!" Roger snapped defensively. "But time over here is…it's weird. I walked around thinking I should go check things out, and it didn't seem like it had been so long, but…"

He stared at me, and I waited expectantly.

"Darren is *bald*," he told me, frowning.

"I—*what?*"

I haven't seen Darren since he graduated, the same school year when Roger died.

"Yep." He nodded firmly, lips pressed tightly. He glanced around the gymnasium, then up at the ceiling. "Bald as Marshall McKay's golf ball." He looked at me then, and his eyes twinkled.

We both burst out laughing.

"Oh, dang!" I cried. "Outside, quick."

I hurried us out the door, down the hall and out to the parking lot in back. I could always claim I'd forgotten something, even though all my equipment was inside, ready to use.

We couldn't quite stop giggling.

Finally, Roger asked, "How old are you, Emma?"

"Twenty-seven," I replied.

Roger shook his head in mock sadness. "Bald at thirty," he mused, then snorted out another giggle.

I gave him a wicked grin. "So was my uncle Ezra," I told him. "You had at least a 50-50 chance."

"Oh, I'd a hundred percent be bald," Roger grinned. "Dad was already losing his hair, but at least he made it past forty! And—oh, yeah." He looked crestfallen.

It must be hard to have everything you ever knew turn out to be a lie, I think. It had just occurred to him that the man he'd called 'Dad' his whole life was not the one who'd provided his genetics.

"This is just crap," he growled. "Anyway, I was going to say that Mom's father and brothers were bald, too."

I sighed. "Yeah," I agreed. "It's total crap, and you would a hundred percent be bald as Mrs. McKay's little nesting egg."

I had no intention of telling Roger what had happened to that poor woman.

"My parents are still together," Roger mused.

"Yeah. I see them now and then."

"Why did she stay?" He didn't seem to need an answer; it was just one of those questions you ask. "She must have been unhappy, to have an affair with an old guy."

"Our parents are older now than Ezra was then," I reminded him.

"Whatever. He was an old guy to her, then. I just…I don't get it."

Well, dear diary, I don't have any answers about people falling in love or having affairs or anything like that. People do things for so many different reasons.

Maybe her husband was so busy he was ignoring her, and she needed attention.

Maybe they were fighting a lot, over money or something.

Maybe she had "daddy issues".

Maybe she was just bored.

Uncle Ezra has been married three times, though, I know that. And he's always been somewhat notorious among the family for being a bit of a playboy.

I once heard my grandpa chastising my uncles Danny and Rob for their deep admiration of Ezra's 'way with the ladies'. "A man who treats a woman like a conquest to be won does the lady no favors, and gains nothing!" he told them. "The woman has been made from a person into a thing, and a possession can give no man true happiness. Ezra will never be a happy man until he learns that a trophy does nothing but sit on a shelf and gather dust, and a *real* woman can't be won. She gives of herself freely, with nothing to gain or give but love."

Danny had chuckled, but Rob gave him a sharp poke. "Dad's right," he said. "If I can win a woman away from the man she's with, *that* is a woman who can be won by someone else away from me. Who needs that?"

Dan's jaw had dropped. Grandpa was smart.

I scoffed now, really understanding that little lesson fully. It would go both ways, of course. A man could as easily be the "prize", to be won over and over.

I suddenly felt sorry for Roger's mother and my Uncle Ezra.

It would really, really be best if his not-real dad never found out.

And you know, whatever the circumstances, stuff happens. Then you have to sort through it and muddle your way to the next thing. It would be easy to judge folks, but I don't know their lives, or their feelings or what it's like to walk in their shoes.

Let God judge. That's his job.

He's welcome to it.

We went back to the auditorium, and Roger went wandering through the growing throng of kids.

Dear diary, let me just tell you that school dances have changed since I was a kid at this school. We used to play records; I think we all brought in our own records and people took turns standing around the record player and changing the tunes.

These kids had a disc jockey, some guy who came in with his own gear and stood up there and did all the work. He announced songs and everything.

Honestly, I feel a little cheated. Ha ha!

One thing that hasn't changed since my Junior High dance days is that the kids still split up unless they actually have a date. The girls were all sitting on the bleachers on one side of the gym, and the boys were on the bleachers on the other side. There were the obvious wallflowers, all alone, and the clique groups who were dateless but at least had a group to hang out with. They moved about in packs, giggling and gossiping.

God, I'm so glad I survived those days. Thank God for Sasha and Martin; I never had to be that lone wallflower after we became friends. I always had someone to sit with while the boys ignored me and didn't ask me to dance.

I had gone tonight with low to medium hopes of doing a lot of dance night photos, but the kids lined up and I worked steadily through the evening. That was nice.

The newspaper's reporter interrupted things about halfway through the festivities and interviewed the students responsible for arranging the fundraiser. I took several pictures of them, then returned to my big camera.

Throughout the event I caught occasional glimpses of Roger, who meandered through the gym, followed a few of the teachers around and swayed on the dancefloor to some older songs.

A couple of times he came into my workspace and poked his head into a photo shoot, grinning mischievously. Trying not to glare at him or otherwise give any indication to the students that something was amiss other than a camera issue, I retook the shots he popped into—just in case.

Honestly, Diary! A ghost with a sense of humor. It's not unheard of. But…I don't get it, that's all. I mean, he was so down when he was alive that he shot himself. Where does this grinning, dancing goof-off come from?

That's what kept going through my mind. Why now? Why not when he was alive, when it likely would have *kept* him alive?

Also…why did it take him this long to find me? My great-grandfather died in 1985, and Grandma—his daughter—died last fall.

I didn't stay for the whole dance; my customer base dwindled and stopped shortly after the interview was done, and I started packing up. Roger hung around, pretending to be helpful.

Of course, my real helper was Fred, who showed up just in time to help carry the bigger things back to my car. He'd begged a ride from Dad, who was happy to drop him off. He listened as I continued to talk to Roger.

"What took you so long, Roger? Why didn't you come to me before?" I asked.

"Emma, I don't know!" Roger shook his head. "I can't tell you how long I've been gone, I can't tell you when my grandfather came, and I can't tell you how long I waited after talking to him before I came to find you."

"Who's Roger?" Fred asked. I frowned at him and shook my head.

"I don't know what happens to other people," Roger continued. He paid no particular attention to my brother as we carefully re-packed the backdrop. "Maybe it was because I offed myself, but I never saw anyone until my grandfather showed up."

"No one?" That seemed wrong to me. *Was* it because he "offed" himself, like he said? Was it some sort of punishment?

If it was, who was responsible for that, and why did they let my great-grandfather see and talk to him?

Diary, I don't like questions like that. They upset me. They kind of piss me off, even.

"Well," Roger said, "it's not like I know a lot of dead people. I never went to a funeral even once in my whole life."

"Oh. Well, that's not a bad thing, I'd say."

"I guess," Roger sighed. "But if I had, maybe I would have…I don't know…thought things over."

I didn't know what to say to that.

"I *have* done a lot of thinking since, though." He sighed again. "A lot."

"Roger," I said, "I would like to help you, but I don't know what it is you want from me." I held up a hand to stop him before he could say anything. "Please, please don't say you want me to ask your mother about Ezra."

"Uncle Ezra?" Fred gasped. "Is he—?"

"No, Fred," I told him. "Later."

Fred glared at me like he was considering shaking me until my teeth rattled, but he backed off.

"Oh, God, no!" Roger cried. "No, nothing like that. But…"

"But, what?" I asked.

"Look, it seems like the town has grown some, and probably not as many people know about you these days…"

"Well, one can hope," I said.

I didn't add that strangers often come up to me with questions, so someone out there must be yacking it up.

"But my family knows."

"Uh…okay. And?"

Yep, I was worried now.

"It would be nice if they knew I was sorry. That I would take it all back if I could."

Well, once again, I didn't know what to say. It's not like I could just jump in my car and drive over to his parents' house and knock on the door. And even if I could…well…boo to that idea!

Fred kept staring at me as we packed up the car. I put my cash box on the back seat, wanting to get a total on the night's intake so I could figure out my donation and take a check back inside before I left.

Oh, man, I just wanted to tell Roger to talk to Fred for a minute and let me think.

If only it were that easy!

After a long silence, Roger said, "Look Emma, I know you can't just go to them and blurt stuff out. But if you should happen to see them somewhere…I mean, you could say something then, couldn't you?"

I sighed deeply. See, it's complicated. Whatever else gets said about me around here, people know enough about it to understand that I see my own family.

I mean, I've made a point of repeating that over and over again, for years! You know, so people would quit asking me to call their long-lost uncle and ask him where he hid the will or something.

I only see family.

So how do I explain seeing Roger?

"I don't know how to bring that up without…I mean… Roger, are you sure you even want me to say anything?" I stared at him beseechingly. "People do know about me, about my family…stuff…"

Roger looked confused, and then understanding filled his face with a startled expression. "Crap!" he said.

"Yeah," I agreed.

"Oh crap! And your brother is listening!"

"Fred doesn't say anything."

"No," Fred said. "Fred says nothing, knows nothing, and sees nothing." He nodded in the general direction of California, as if it might be Roger.

It wasn't even close.

"Look," I said. "If Grandpa knew to look for you, I have to think Uncle Ezra knows you're gone. And in that case, he must have kept in touch somehow…"

I was thinking out loud. And not very well, probably.

"Maybe I should just—"

"No," Roger said. "I don't know him. I never even *heard* of him before…you know. I don't care if he knows anything at all about me. You know, even if it's not his fault that I never knew about him. Because maybe my mom didn't want…hell, of course she didn't, why would she?"

Roger stood in the parking lot next to my car, staring at his feet.

I noticed that he was wearing white Ked's high-tops, and that there was a splash of blood across the toe of the right one.

I wish to God I had never seen that!

Finally, he looked up at me. "I don't know what I was thinking," he said. "I should never have come here."

"Roger, don't—"

He was gone.

"—leave." I stared at the empty space where he'd been. Then I stared at Fred. "Well, dang!" I cried. "Now what?"

"What just happened here?" Fred demanded.

Well, diary, I am a real pain in the butt, because instead of telling Fred the story right then, I made him wait while I tallied up my take, calculated my expenses and then wrote a check for the fundraiser donation. Then I made him go back inside the school with me to deliver it to the donation booth.

After that I let him drive us to Burger a Go-Go for Old English chips and a shake. Then we sat in the car and indulged our salt and sugar cravings while I told him the story.

"That's messed up," Fred declared, when I'd finished the tale. "What are you going to do?"

"What can I do?" I demanded. "He took off! I'm not making any decisions about this without him."

"What if he never comes back?" Fred protested.

"Oh. My. **God**!" I groaned loudly and banged the back of my head on the car's headrest. "This is so unfair."

"Yeah, no kidding." Fred chomped a chip and then slurped vanilla shake through his straw. "Mmm. Do you think he'll come back?"

"Oh, man, how should I know?" I was so frustrated, even chocolate wasn't helping.

"Should we ask Mom?"

"Oh, dear Lord, save me from impossible questions!" I begged. "No, no, we can't ask Mom."

"Why?"

"Well, because she…I mean, it would be so…he's her…I don't know!"

"Well, that's logical," Fred said dryly. Then he laughed. "And specific."

"Oh, shut up."

Fred handed me his food and shake and started the car. "I'm taking you home," he said.

"Wanna stay the night?" I asked. "Help develop some photos?"

"Sure!" Fred is always enthusiastic about photography and loves the development process. When my asthma is acting up, he's my go-to guy. Masks and gowns are a big help, but there are times when it's just not enough.

Here's the thing, though. I hate paying someone else to develop my film and I really hate waiting. I want to see the photos ASAP. So, hurrah for Fred.

Tonight was not a problem asthma night, though, and that's great.

Diary, you will never believe this in a million years!

We got the darkroom set up and started going through the orders one by one. I managed to get some great pictures tonight, and I was feeling pretty proud.

Then we discovered one that seemed off. There was some sort of cloudy image on the film.

"What is this?" Fred asked. We both peered through a magnifying glass at the image on the film, but couldn't figure it out, so we proceeded to develop the print, and when we looked at the photo, it looked like the boy in the picture had some sort of strange shadow.

The next photo was the same couple, but that print was flawless.

Then I remembered that Roger had jokingly stepped into the shot, and I had done a re-shoot.

Eagerly, we went through the other photos and found two more with those strange shadows, followed by flawless prints of the same couples.

"This is incredible!" Fred cried. "Do you think it's Roger?"

"I'm pretty sure it is," I replied. My stomach was fluttering with excitement. I didn't want to say anything yet, though, so we finished up with the job and got all the photos printed.

I don't usually take up this task late at night, but as you may recall, Mom has the kids. Why not take advantage of uninterrupted time and a helpful assistant?

Besides, I was beside myself trying not to get my hopes up about something that might not have happened.

When we finished in the darkroom, Fred was babbling away about the shadows on the three photographs, wondering out loud if they could be sharpened up or enlarged.

Finally, I could hold in my own excitement no longer. "Fred," I said, "run up and grab my bag, will you? I think it's still in the car."

He did as I asked.

Now, remember that Polaroid test shot I told you about? The one I took when I started setting up for the evening?

I hadn't bothered to look at it. I had the shot I needed for set-up and just threw everything in my bag.

When Fred gave me the bag I pulled out the photos and quickly sorted through them.

And there it was!

Yeah, diary. You can see Roger! It's not super clear, and he's transparent—you can see the backdrop behind him—but if someone who knew him ever saw it, they could recognize him.

Now, I don't know whether to be stoked or terrified. All I know is it's too late to call Sasha, and I had to tell someone RIGHT NOW, so you were elected.

Oh, and Fred is over the moon, and won't shut up, so I don't think we'll be sleeping any time soon.

I don't know what happens next, dear diary. I can't go see Roger's mother. I can't. Not without talking to Roger.

I'm not going public with these photos, either.

It's not that I wouldn't love to, you know. Finally, I would have something to back up my claims, you know?

Plus, the scientific implications are just…astounding, really.

But—

Can you imagine the repercussions? Not to mention all the old wounds that would be open. It's amazing and wonderful, yes, and I have GOT to share with Sasha, but I don't want anyone to get hurt.

So, for now, that's my story.

I saw a ghost. And now, Fred has seen a ghost, too!

Yes!

Until we meet again!

Em

# Afterward

Well, it is clearly not the end of the story.

Certainly, Emma isn't content with how this day ended. She's been given just enough information to spark her imagination and start her asking questions that she actually has a good chance of getting answers to, if she dares to pursue the issue.

The problem is, time is funny over there. How long will it take Roger to decide what *he* wants? After all, it is his story, not Emma's.

What if, as Fred suggested, he never comes back?

The dilemma Emma faces is that there are living, breathing individuals who can be touched by this story. Some may be enlightened, some may be hurt.

Nevertheless, she wants to know things. She wants to know, first of all, if anyone else besides Roger's mother and her own great-uncle Ezra know about the affair and Roger's parentage.

She can't ask either of them! Not without Roger's cooperation. What sort of person would that make her?

It's a conundrum.

Since Emma can't demand that Roger come back, all she can do is wait. It could be a day, or a year. Or never.

In the meantime, there are more ghosts….

And Emma will be there to talk to them.

*Not* The End
May 14, 2018